Dear Parents and Educators,

Welcome to Penguin Young Readers! As parents and educators, you know that each child develops at his or her own pace—in terms of speech, critical thinking, and, of course, reading. Penguin Young Readers recognizes this fact. As a result, each Penguin Young Readers book is assigned a traditional easy-to-read level (1–4) as well as a Guided Reading Level (A–P). Both of these systems will help you choose the right book for your child. Please refer to the back of each book for specific leveling information. Penguin Young Readers features esteemed authors and illustrators, stories about favorite characters, fascinating nonfiction, and more!

The Teeny-Tiny Woman

LEVEL 2

GUIDED READING LEVEL **H**

This book is perfect for a **Progressing Reader** who:
• can figure out unknown words by using picture and context clues;
• can recognize beginning, middle, and ending sounds;
• can make and confirm predictions about what will happen in the text; and
• can distinguish between fiction and nonfiction.

Here are some **activities** you can do during and after reading this book:
• Sight Words: Sight words are frequently used words that readers know instantly, on sight. Knowing these words helps children develop into efficient readers. As you read the story, have the child point out the sight words listed below.

got	into	out	said	she	went
her	one	put	saw	walk	when

• Retelling: Have the child tell you what happened in the beginning, middle, and end of the story. Then talk about the last sentence in the book. Does the child think the woman used a teeny-tiny voice? Ask the child to pretend that he/she is the teeny-tiny woman and read that sentence out loud.

Remember, sharing the love of reading with a child is the best gift you can give!

—Bonnie Bader, EdM
  Penguin Young Readers program

*Penguin Young Readers are leveled by independent reviewers applying the standards developed by Irene Fountas and Gay Su Pinnell in *Matching Books to Readers: Using Leveled Books in Guided Reading*, Heinemann, 1999.

Penguin Young Readers
Published by the Penguin Group
Penguin Group (USA) Inc., 375 Hudson Street, New York, New York 10014, USA
Penguin Group (Canada), 90 Eglinton Avenue East, Suite 700, Toronto, Ontario M4P 2Y3, Canada
(a division of Pearson Penguin Canada Inc.)
Penguin Books Ltd., 80 Strand, London WC2R 0RL, England
Penguin Group Ireland, 25 St. Stephen's Green, Dublin 2, Ireland (a division of Penguin Books Ltd.)
Penguin Group (Australia), 250 Camberwell Road, Camberwell, Victoria 3124, Australia
(a division of Pearson Australia Group Pty. Ltd.)
Penguin Books India Pvt. Ltd., 11 Community Centre, Panchsheel Park, New Delhi—110 017, India
Penguin Group (NZ), 67 Apollo Drive, Rosedale, Auckland 0632, New Zealand
(a division of Pearson New Zealand Ltd.)
Penguin Books (South Africa) (Pty.) Ltd., 24 Sturdee Avenue,
Rosebank, Johannesburg 2196, South Africa

Penguin Books Ltd., Registered Offices: 80 Strand, London WC2R 0RL, England

Library of Congress Control Number: 94043813

ISBN 978-0-14-037625-8   10 9 8 7 6 5 4 3 2 1

The Teeny-Tiny Woman

retold by Harriet Ziefert
illustrated by Laura Rader

Penguin Young Readers
An Imprint of Penguin Group (USA) Inc.

Once upon a time,

a teeny-tiny woman

lived in a teeny-tiny house.

One nice day,

the teeny-tiny woman

went for a teeny-tiny walk.

The teeny-tiny woman

walked a teeny-tiny way.

She opened a teeny-tiny gate.

She went into

a teeny-tiny graveyard.

In the teeny-tiny graveyard,
the teeny-tiny woman
saw a teeny-tiny bone
on a teeny-tiny grave.

The teeny-tiny woman said,
"This teeny-tiny bone will make
a teeny-tiny soup for my
teeny-tiny supper."

The teeny-tiny woman

put the teeny-tiny bone

into her teeny-tiny pocket.

She went back to

her teeny-tiny house.

When she got home,

the teeny-tiny woman was sleepy.

So she went upstairs

to her teeny-tiny bedroom.

She put the teeny-tiny bone

into a teeny-tiny cabinet.

The teeny-tiny woman
got into her teeny-tiny bed
and went to sleep.

A teeny-tiny voice

woke up the teeny-tiny woman.

"Give me my bone!"

it said.

The teeny-tiny woman was

a teeny-tiny bit scared.

She hid her teeny-tiny head

under the covers

and went to sleep again.

The teeny-tiny voice woke up

the teeny-tiny woman again.

24

"Give me my bone!"

it said, a teeny-tiny bit louder.

The teeny-tiny woman

was a teeny-tiny bit

more scared.

So she hid her head

a teeny-tiny bit more

under the covers.

Then the teeny-tiny voice said

a teeny-tiny bit louder still,

"*Give me my bone!*"

This time the teeny-tiny woman

stuck her head out and said,

"Take it!"